P9-DNC-843

9/95 Brodart 14.95

The Princess and the Beggar

A KOREAN FOLKTALE

adapted and illustrated by
ANNE SIBLEY O'BRIEN

POLLARD SCHOOL LIBRARY

SCHOLASTIC INC.
New York

Thanks to my parents;
O.B., Ed, Sue, Natalie, Norman, Emily, Kenneth,
David, Nancy, Phoebe, Hyun-hee, Young-chul,
and the members of my writing group.

Copyright © 1993 by Anne Sibley O'Brien.
All rights reserved. Published by Scholastic Inc.
SCHOLASTIC HARDCOVER is a registered trademark of Scholastic Inc.

No part of this publication may be reproduced in whole or in part,
or stored in a retrieval system, or transmitted in any form or
by any means, electronic, mechanical, photocopying, recording,
or otherwise, without written permission of the publisher.
For information regarding permission write to Scholastic Inc.,
730 Broadway, New York, NY 10003.

Library of Congress Cataloging-in-Publication Data

O'Brien, Anne Sibley.
The princess and the beggar : a Korean folktale / adapted and
illustrated by Anne Sibley O'Brien.
p.   cm.
Summary: A sad princess finds happiness after marrying a beggar.
ISBN 0-590-46092-7
[1. Folklore — Korea.]   I. Title.
PZ8.1.O227Pr   1992
398.21 — dc20
[E]
92-11988
—   CIP
AC

12 11 10 9 8 7 6 5 4 3 2 1   3 4 5 6 7 8/9
Printed in the U.S.A.   36
First Scholastic printing, April 1993

Designed by Marijka Kostiw

The illustrations in this book
were created with pastels
and colored pencils.

This book is dedicated with love and appreciation
to my Korean brothers and sisters —
  Hahn Jae-chul
  Kim Hyun-hee
  Young Hobbie
and in memory of Choi Hwa-wook.

A.S.O.

In an ancient kingdom a craggy mountain rises out of the mist. Peony Peak, it is called. Below, a wide green river valley stretches down to the sea. Nestled in the curve of the river is the ancient walled city of Pyung-yang, where…once upon a time, there lived a king whose youngest and favorite daughter was known to all as the Weeping Princess.

On a bright spring morning, the great wooden palace gates creaked open. "Make way! Make way for the royal family!" bellowed a herald. "The queen and her daughters travel to the Spring Pavilion!"

But as the procession reached the market at East Gate, the royal family was jostled by the boisterous crowd. "Make way! Make way for the royal family!" the herald repeated, but the market did not give way. Chickens squawked, dogs barked, hawkers bawled, buyers bickered, all at the top of their lungs.

Suddenly the bearers of the third sedan chair halted. "Yaaah, clumsy dog! Out of the way!" the herald yelled. The youngest princess peeked out from behind the brocade flap. A filthy boy lay sprawled in the mud.

"It's only the beggar boy, Ondal!" said the herald. "Hey, Pabo! Pabo Ondal! Move out of the way!" he yelled, kicking the boy aside. The princess was too frightened to protest, but tears of sympathy welled up in her eyes.

As they alighted at the pavilion, her sister teased, "There she goes again, our Weeping Princess!"

The princess sobbed harder. Her mother sighed. "Why does she cry about everything? What man will want a wife who cries all the time?!"

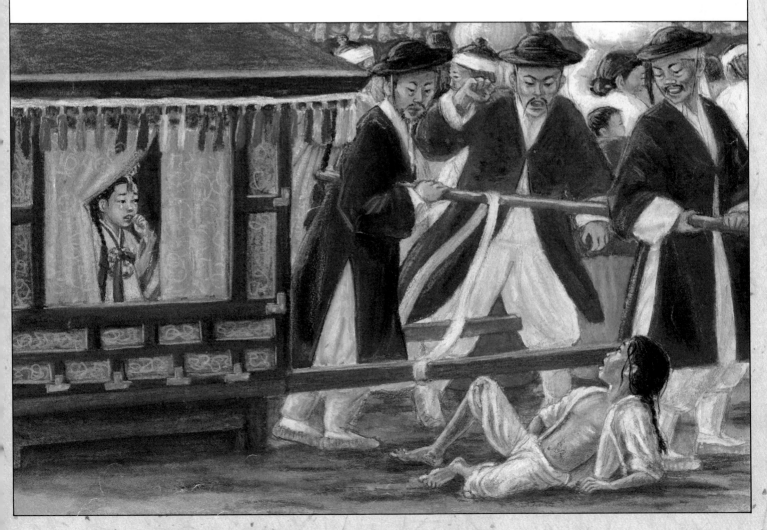

Six summers passed. The winter snows lined the river-banks with ice, and the northern winds were bitter. In the marketplace vendors huddled over their fires and exchanged stories about the beggar, Ondal.

"He lives among the creatures in the mountains," said one. "No better than an animal," agreed another. In time, their wild stories reached even the ears of the king.

On the first morning of the new year, the youngest princess gathered with her sisters and brothers in the Grand Palace. But as she made her bow before the king, she tripped and stumbled. Tears silently spilled down her cheeks.

"Heh, heh! What's this noise? Who's crying on the first day of the new year?" teased the king. "Speak up! Speak up!" But when the princess remained silent, the king frowned with displeasure. "This daughter is impossible! If she keeps crying at every little thing, we'll... marry her off to the beggar, Pabo Ondal!" His humor once more restored, the king chuckled at his joke.

The queen turned pale at his words. "Do not speak of such things on the first day of the new year," she rebuked him.

But it was too late. Everyone in court had heard the king's joke. From that moment, the Weeping Princess had no peace. There was always someone nearby to tease, "Oh, ho! You'll be the wife of Pabo Ondal! The king himself has said so!"

"Did you know he wears animal skins and sleeps in a cave?" "He tears his meat raw from the bones!"

The princess only cried harder. She hid in the palace library, and consoled herself by reading her favorite poems and adventurous tales of dragons and tigers. But for fear of ridicule, she kept her studies a secret

Dragon

When the princess was in her sixteenth year, the king announced to the court, "It is time for the youngest princess to marry. I have arranged a most excellent match with the son of noble Ko."

The princess considered her future life as a noblewoman—running a household under her mother-in-law's direction, with only frivolous parties and court gossip for entertainment. No solitude, no secret studies. "I will be miserable," she thought.

"Sir...I cannot accept," the princess whispered.

"You *cannot*? What do you mean, you cannot?" shouted the king. "I have arranged a fine match for which any sensible girl would be grateful! You say you *cannot*? You *will* obey me!" he thundered.

In desperation, the princess searched for an excuse. "I most humbly beg your pardon, most Honored Father...but before I wed the son of noble Ko, I...I would be the wife of Pabo Ondal!"

The king's eyes bulged like a warrior demon's, his eyebrows bristling. "The wife of Pabo Ondal?! What nonsense is this?"

"But, Esteemed Father," she pressed on recklessly, "*you* said you would marry me to Pabo Ondal. How can the king go back on his word?"

"Go then to your Pabo Ondal before you bring more shame upon your family!" Enraged beyond reason, the king banished his favorite daughter from the palace.

POLLARD SCHOOL LIBRARY

Just before dawn, the princess left the palace alone and on foot for the first time. She carried one small bundle, a parting gift of gold pieces from the queen.

The princess walked in the direction of Peony Peak, for Pabo Ondal's hut was said to be at the foot of the mountain path.

At sundown, she reached a clearing where a shabby straw-roofed hut stood alone. The princess wiped away tears of exhaustion mingled with fear. She jumped at the sound of a voice, raw and grating.

"Why do you weep?"

"I have come to be the wife of Ondal," the princess whispered.

"Why do you mock me?" the voice asked harshly.

"If Ondal will not have me," the princess replied humbly, "then I have nowhere to go. I have been banished from my home."

A man with matted hair and ragged clothes stepped up from behind her. Slowly he reached out and gently brushed away her tears with his rough fingers.

That year the rains washed in summer's brilliant greens in the clearing at the foot of Peony Peak. The princess shyly followed Ondal as he gathered roots and hunted in the forest. Ondal watched as she patiently stitched fine linen garments to replace his tattered clothing. In time— as they planted, tended, and mended together, they learned not to fear each other.

In the winter, deep snows filled the mountain pass. On the long dark evenings, the princess recited her favorite poems to Ondal. She also taught him how to read and write.

The princess marveled at the quickness with which Ondal learned. She remembered his many kindnesses to her and his gentleness with the creatures of the forest. "How terrible that the village people call him a wild beast and an idiot! Those who mock him shall learn the truth," she decided.

On the first warm day, the princess placed two gold pieces in Ondal's palm. "Husband, you must go to the market in the city and buy a horse. The horse may be weak and lame as long as it is of royal lineage."

Ondal was reluctant to do her bidding for he feared the scorn of the villagers. But the princess persuaded him. "See how we both have changed. You are no longer Pabo Ondal the beggar and I am no Weeping Princess."

Ondal returned the next nightfall, leading a scrawny, unkempt horse.

The princess and Ondal cared tenderly for the horse. When the horse grew strong enough, the princess began Ondal's riding lessons.

Another year passed, and spring once again came to the clearing. One morning the princess turned to Ondal. "Husband," said she. "On the third day of the third month, the king holds the Festival of the Hunters. This year, you are ready to join the hunt." Ondal protested, but once again the princess persuaded him to do her bidding.

At the king's hunting festival, a mysterious rider dressed as a commoner startled the noble huntsmen with his fearless exploits. But before they could discover his identity, he disappeared. The curious onlookers talked among themselves.

"On the Full Moon Night of the fifth month, the king will hold the Festival of the Scholars. Surely a nobleman of such talent will enter the poetry contest."

News of the competition reached even the hut at the foot of Peony Peak.

"Husband, you must compete with the scholars," the princess told Ondal. A third time, Ondal agreed to do his wife's bidding. He was overjoyed when the princess prepared to accompany him into the city.

They arrived in the capital on the afternoon of the festival. The sounds of drums and flutes and gongs filled the city streets, now crowded with masked dancers, farmers' bands, and peddlers selling spring wine and sweets to hungry spectators. Ondal and the princess wandered the festive streets until dusk.

As evening fell, Ondal joined the scholars at the Lotus Pavilion. Only he was dressed in commoner's clothing. The noblemen protested. "Everyone knows peasants neither read nor write!"

Ondal silenced them. "What then have you to fear?"

When the moon rose to brighten the darkened sky, the crowd hushed. Ondal bowed his head in contemplation. He prepared his ink. With firm strokes, he brushed the characters of his poem.

"Such simplicity!" "Such swiftness!" "Such strength!" whispered the judges in admiration.

The first judge lifted Ondal's
scroll and read for all to hear:
 "On the wild mountain
 a lone orchid,
 filled with dew,
 trembles.
 The drops spill,
 fall on a withered seedling.
 The dying pine stirs to life."

The onlookers broke into applause. Standing among them, the princess wiped a tear from the corner of her eye.

The king clapped loudest of all. He called the winner of the poetry contest before him.

"Are you not the skilled huntsman from the hunting festival?" the king demanded.

"Royal Highness," replied Ondal, "I am he."

"What of your common appearance? How is it possible that you have mastered the royal arts?" questioned the king.

"Most noble sir, all that I have learned, I owe to my esteemed wife."

"Oh, ho!" exclaimed the king. "Such a woman of talent I would like to see! Have her come forward at once!" he ordered.

The princess approached the Lotus Pavilion and stood beside Ondal. She bowed with perfect grace before the king. "Royal Highness," she said, "in earlier days my husband was known by the name of Pabo Ondal."

The news spread quickly through the crowd. "The banished princess has returned!" "The stranger is he who was called Pabo Ondal!" "A peasant has won the king's poetry contest!"

Finally the king spoke. "My daughter has returned," he proclaimed, "bringing me a new son worthy of honor. You have won the King's favor. What do you ask of me?"

At Ondal's nod, the princess replied, "Honored Father. We are but simple folk. We ask only to serve you when you have need."

And so it came to pass in the years that followed, Ondal's services to the king were many and great, but his happiness awaited him at the foot of Peony Peak.

ABOUT THIS BOOK

The folktale, Pabo Ondal (loosely translated "Idiot Ondal"), has delighted generations of Koreans. Several written versions place the story in the late sixth century, during the reign of King Pyungkang of the Koguryo Dynasty. I have retained the setting of Pyung-yang, the capital of Koguryo, which is now located in North Korea. Since there is so little information about Koguryo society, the pictures and text in this book reflect the clothing, hairstyles, architecture, and customs of the Yi Dynasty (1392–1910), the basis for what is currently known as "traditional" Korean culture.

In this book, you can tell the difference between Korean peasants and nobility by their clothing, shoes, and hats. During the Yi Dynasty, noblewomen dressed in fine silks and brocades. All noblemen wore hats and the court officials wore deeply colored brocade robes and boots. The peasants wore plainly woven garments in white and muted colors, and shoes made of straw.

Children were the exception. Families of all classes enjoyed dressing their children in brightly colored clothing. Both girls and boys wore their hair long, in one braid down the back. After marriage women wound their braid into a knot and inserted a hairpin through it. Married men pulled their hair into a top-knot. A male peasant often tied a white cloth strip around his head like a sweatband.

The designs for the seals found on the endpapers are derived from folk symbols. Some represent the four directions, the sun and the moon, heaven and earth, or flowers like the lotus and the plum blossom.

Pabo (PAH-bo) means fool, idiot, or stupid. Ondal (ON-dahl) is a given name. Korean vowels are pronounced similarly to Spanish vowels: soft "a" as in "father"; long "o" as in "over."

A.S.O.

398.21
OBR   O'Brien, Anne Sibley

        The princess and
        the beggar

DUE DATE	BRODART	06/93	14.95
10·1 MAY 06 1996			
10:25 OCT 28			
APR 26 JUN 09 199			
5-6 OCT 24 199			
JUN 1 MAR 25 1998			
OCT 12 MAY 3 1999			
OCT 28 19 MAY 02 2001			
NOV 30 199 APR 30 2002			
JUN 0 MAY 16			
MAR 18 1996			
APR 01 1996			

POLLARD SCHOOL LIBRARY